HOLLOW INSIDE

ASAKO OTANI was born in Chiba Prefecture in 1990. Her debut novel, *Hollow Inside,* won the 2022 Subaru Literary Prize.

GINNY TAPLEY TAKEMORI is the prize-winning translator of Sayaka Murata's *Convenience Store Woman, Earthlings,* and *Life Ceremony,* as well as many of her short stories, and other celebrated authors including Kyoko Nakajima and Ryu Murakami.

HOLLOW INSIDE

ASAKO OTANI

Translated from the Japanese by

GINNY TAPLEY TAKEMORI

PUSHKIN PRESS

Pushkin Press
Somerset House, Strand
London WC2R 1LA

GARANDOU by Asako Otani

First published in Japan in 2023 by SHUEISHA Inc., Tokyo.

English edition published by arrangement with
Shueisha Inc., Tokyo
Through Japan UNI Agency, Inc., Tokyo

First published by Pushkin Press in 2026

ISBN 13: 978-1-80568-001-7

A CIP catalogue record for this title is available from the British Library

The authorised representative in the EEA is eucomply OÜ,
Pärnu mnt. 139b-14, 11317, Tallinn, Estonia,
hello@eucompliancepartner.com, +33757690241

Designed and typeset by Tetragon, London
Printed and bound in the United Kingdom by Clays Ltd, Elcograf S.p.A.

Pushkin Press is committed to a sustainable future for our business, our readers and our planet. This book is made from paper from forests that support responsible forestry.

www.pushkinpress.com

3 5 7 9 8 6 4 2

HOLLOW INSIDE

SUGANUMA WAS in the living room making dead dogs.

The 3D printer on the cabinet was making a hell of a racket as it squeezed out molten white filament. It was the size of a smallish Buddhist home altar, a bare-bones model with exposed arm and head. It wasn't so much futuristic as reminiscent of a paper guillotine gathering dust in the back of the school art room.

An H-shaped structure stood atop a base, with a small box-shaped head attached to the crossbar. This head was inching its way from side to side, its motor screaming. A nozzle on the head was extruding filament onto the base, and the figure of a dog was gradually emerging from the feet up.

A photograph of the dog stood on the edge of the cabinet. It was already dead. They all were.

Suganuma's 3D printer was a bit too noisy for home use. At first it had been in her room, but she couldn't sleep when it was running and had moved it to the cabinet in the corner of the living room. Now, as she stood facing the corner while she operated it, it was as though she too was being driven out of the apartment.

I stood behind her stuffing my breakfast bread roll into my mouth. I didn't bother about the crumbs falling onto my white blouse. I could gather them up and throw them away when I'd finished. Suganuma had been complaining of deteriorating eyesight lately, and now and then stood back from the machine to observe the details of the emerging figure. Her oversized T-shirt revealed the contours of her skinny body, and all the bumps of her spine stood out starkly when she rounded her back. Her hair, carelessly gathered into a ponytail, was splitting at the ends for lack of moisture and nutrients. From behind, her thin body didn't look firm and well toned, it just looked frail.

As soon as cheap 3D printers hit the market, Suganuma had bought one, thinking she could make some money with it. She had tried various things, but the best-paying job turned out to be making custom dog figurines. She would be sent photos of pet dogs that had died, and would tweak templates of particular breeds to produce models that were the spitting image of those beloved pets. The plain white figures she made would then be sent out for colouring before being delivered to the respective owners. It was cheaper and easier than taxidermy, and popular with owners who couldn't bear the thought of skinning their pet.

I picked up what looked like a reject figure that was lying on the floor. It was of a chihuahua, hollow inside and surprisingly light. The threadlike filament had become tangled around its body, as though enveloping it in a spider's web. Could the grieving owner get some measure of comfort from holding this hollow figure made to look like their pet? I couldn't even begin to imagine it.

"We're down to our last roll of toilet paper," Suganuma said suddenly, without taking her eyes off the machine.

"I'll get some on my way home from work, if I remember."

"Please."

I put the figurine of the chihuahua down on the low table. The filament had wound around its legs so that it was unable to stand properly, and it toppled forward onto its nose.

I'd forgotten about the crumbs from my breakfast and they scattered over the floor as I left for work.

I couldn't get a seat on the commuter train, but it wasn't too packed as it was headed away from Tokyo. As I held on to an overhead strap and braced my legs, I caught sight of my dim reflection in the window. A plain woman just shy of forty in a grey skirt. I had the feeling that by blurring my focus I could be completely assimilated into the jostle of strangers around me on the swaying train. I crossed my eyes slightly and concentrated on erasing my existence.

Our office was some distance from the business district around the station, on the fourth floor of a cheap-looking building that housed various stores, offices and restaurants. The layout was old-fashioned, with the desks arranged in five islands and the group leaders in the seat of honour at the head of each. It was a cosy little printing company with just a production department and printing plant in addition to this office.

There were about twenty dull old men in this dull old office crammed with stuff, but I didn't know whether they were dull from working here or whether they had chosen this job because they were dull in the first place. There were also several women employees wearing make-up that seemed to indicate a strong resistance to being tainted by the environment, but I myself probably blended right in by now, having started working there seventeen years ago, straight after graduation.

I arrived at my desk just as Yoshida, who sat opposite me, pulled his bottom desk drawer open with a clatter and threw his shoulder bag into it.

"Mornin'," he muttered without moving his mouth so you could barely catch what he said.

I muttered a similar greeting and sat down, but then noticed that something in my field of vision was different from usual. Through the acrylic desk shield I saw that Yoshida was wearing a white polo shirt. Until now, he'd always worn a white shirt buttoned right up to his neck.

It had been decided that male employees could wear polo shirts from May, but it was only now the rainy season was over and it was getting really hot that they were starting to wear them. The shirt clung tightly to Yoshida's chubby body, and it had some kind of silhouette motif on the left breast. I'd thought it was a Ralph Lauren horse logo, but while it was extremely similar, it was a motif I hadn't seen before. My screen brightened as my computer started up, but I couldn't take my eyes off Yoshida's brand-new polo shirt. What was that motif? The tall, thin silhouette looked a bit like a stain, with jagged contours.

A pop-up window displaying today's schedule appeared on the screen, and I finally managed to drag my eyes away from the polo shirt.

The "New Season Drinks Party" at 16:00 caught my eye. Oh yeah, I'd forgotten about that. I quietly closed the schedule, resisting the urge to click my tongue. Yoshida wiped the sweat from his forehead with a carefully folded handkerchief.

My job came under Accounts.

I was the second longest old-timer in the department. I'd already seen most of the problems that my colleagues got all worked up about, and as I always showed them how we'd solved them in the past they'd started calling me Hirai-sensei, as though I were some kind of teacher or something.

If I were to leave this company, I doubted whether I would find another job where anyone would appreciate me. There had been a time when the company got lots of emails and leaflets advertising business streamlining and systematization, but I'd quietly binned them all. I was scared I'd be out of a job if we ever computerized the office.

The drinks party in the meeting room next door started bang on time. I stayed at my desk, pretending that I had too much work to do. Once a year, Accounts and General Affairs would get together for a party in the meeting room, ordering in catered food and sending some office juniors out to buy a load of drinks. It had been put on hold during the COVID-19 pandemic, but unfortunately they'd started it up again on a smaller scale this year.

I clicked the update button, and the inbox on the accounts system showed up empty. "No new tasks for Ms Hirai," it said. I'd finished all my work for the day.

Of the five work islands in the office, two were occupied by the Accounts division, and a few of my colleagues were still at their desks, too. Next to me, my boss was busy as always, banging away furiously on his keyboard, his face lit up by the screen.

The hubbub coming from the meeting room was getting pretty loud. Despite the noise, though, you couldn't make out any conversations through the single wall separating us. It was as though all the threads of conversation had been unravelled, mixed up, and stuffed back into a homogenous sound that was rapidly getting denser.

One of the younger employees had recently married, so no doubt they were the centre of attention at the party today. I looked down at the veins standing out on the back of my hand resting aimlessly on the mouse, and wondered when I had started feeling so out of place at work drinks parties.

People began filtering back out of the meeting room, dragging the party air along with them. The smell of fried food hung in the air, and I looked up to see Yoshida sit down at his desk.

"Oh, Hirai-san, are you busy?" I heard someone say behind me.

I looked round to see Mrs Kondo standing there holding a tray loaded with cans of beer and cocktails. Mrs Kondo was the number one old-timer in the office, my senpai, and unlike me she had the title of section manager. I had learned everything about my job in Accounts from her.

"Yes, um... I want to finish this task today."

Mrs Kondo had worn the same short hair and black-rimmed glasses for over ten years. It had become her trademark style.

"Really? Well, take some of these drinks home with you, will you? There's quite a lot left over from the party," she said, putting the tray down on my desk.

"Okay then."

I took a canned cocktail. The surface of the can was covered in droplets of moisture, which slid down the gap between the palm of my hand and the can.

"Take as many as you like. Not that I want to burden you with them."

She still didn't make any move to pick up the tray, so I took a can of beer and placed it next to the other one.

"I never knew you drank beer!"

"Oh, it's not for me, it's for my flatmate."

She froze, and her eyes grew exaggeratedly round behind her glasses.

"Ohhhhh... you live with someone?" A second later, she rested her hand on my shoulder and said excitedly, "No way, it's the first I've heard of this. Since when?"

"About four months, I guess."

"Now I want to go out for a drink with you and hear all about it, Ms Hirai. How about this evening?"

She crinkled her eyes in a smile and peered into my face. The snaggle tooth she normally tried to hide was sticking out from under her top lip.

"Er, well..." I smiled vaguely and looked down.

Finally she picked up the tray. "I'm sorry for interrupting your work. Do come to the next drinks party, though. Well then, I'll be off home now."

"Have a good evening."

"Thanks. You too."

I rotated my chair slightly so that I was facing my computer again. I kept aimlessly opening and closing windows, but however hard I searched there wasn't any work for me. Suddenly Yoshida's polo shirt came back into my field of vision. That motif on his left breast. I had a quick flutter of inspiration, as though a breeze had blown through my brain. Could that silhouette be of one of Japan's prefectures? I pretended to be absorbed in the computer screen as I stared at his chest again. I had no idea which prefecture it was, but that was what it looked like.

Yes, that was definitely what it was. It was tall and thin, curved around slightly to the right. But which prefecture was it?

I was about to open a map of Japan in my browser when Yoshida suddenly pushed his chair back and bent forward to open the bottom drawer of his desk. Then he stood up, holding his shoulder bag, and gave a slight bow to the island of desks before leaving.

It was already dark by the time I left the office. Not so long ago it had still been light when I left work on time, but as the elevator doors opened I was struck by the intensity of the blackness before me. The moment I stepped into it, my body blended in. We were only a fifteen-minute walk from the bustle of Yokohama Station, yet the streets here were surprisingly deserted and dark. The inky asphalt melded with the night, illuminated only by the occasional trickle of light from a street lamp.

My bag was heavy with the two cans in it, and I kept shifting it from one hand to the other. I recalled how delighted Mrs Kondo had been upon learning that I was living with someone, almost as if it were her own situation. She had a reputation within the company for being friendly, and she was sweet to me, too, even though I was so bad at socializing.

But actually, I thought, Mrs Kondo wouldn't be so delighted if she knew the truth. I was living with Suganuma, a forty-two-year-old woman.

"How about living together?" Suganuma had asked me last autumn.

She'd taken me out to a popular izakaya and had casually come out with this over our fried chicken and salad. The pandemic had died down by then, and the izakaya was full.

"You what?" I snorted, thinking she was drunk.

"Would you like to share an apartment? We'd be able to get a bigger place and cut down on living expenses, as well as share the housework."

She was more talkative than normal, and her face was unusually flushed even below the line of thickly applied blusher.

"Of course, we'll have separate bedrooms. And you can leave any time you want. Oh, and I should make it clear, I'm not coming on to you at all."

I frowned. Hearing her go on so confidently was scaring me a bit. "I could understand it if we were both young, but... are you serious?"

"There's no law against women in their forties living together, you know."

"But it's not normal either," I said, taking a sip of my lemon sour. "And I'm only thirty-eight, by the way."

"Oops, sorry about that," she said, and casually picked up an edamame pod. "Hirai, when you were a kid, what did you want to be?"

What was she getting at? When I didn't answer, she chewed on the edamame and went on, "I wanted to be a firefighter. I thought they were just the coolest ever."

I frowned, not knowing where she was going with this. Staring at the lip of her beer glass, she finally got to the point.

"The contract for my flat is coming up for renewal. I was thinking about moving for the first time in ages."

"I see."

"The place I'm in now only has one room and a tiny kitchen. I've been working for over twenty years and thought that by now I'd be able to afford somewhere with an open-plan kitchen-living-room and separate bedroom, but the rents in town are too high. The only places I could just about afford would be in wooden buildings or properties built decades ago before the current standards came in, or so far from the station you'd have to take a bus to get there."

I stared at the remains of a squeezed lemon on the table. Part of me wondered whether Suganuma had invited me out tonight just to put this proposal to me.

"Can you believe it? Not only did I fail to become a firefighter, I can't even afford to live in a decent one-bedroom flat. I graduated in the middle of a job drought and could only get work through a temp agency at first, but I studied hard and finally managed to get a permanent job after ten years, then worked my ass off for another ten years, and still I can't even afford a one-bedroom flat. I just can't go on like this."

I could see what she meant.

"With the two of us sharing, we could split the rent, and the cost of food and electricity and stuff would be a lot easier to manage, too."

"Why not just get married?"

"No way I'll ever get married. Not after experiencing the quagmire of my parents' divorce. You know that."

I nodded without saying anything. She was always going on about how marriage was a gamble where the odds were overwhelmingly stacked against you.

"If you just want more space you could buy a place, couldn't you? Friends who own their own homes all live in really nice places."

"Yeah, I guess."

"Right?" I said, sure of myself, and reached for my lemon sour. The ice had melted and the remaining half-glass tasted watery.

"I'm lonely," Suganuma said with resignation. "Working at home during the pandemic brought it home to me. I'd go the whole day without speaking to anyone. You were the only person I ever got to see, Hirai."

There was nothing I could say to that. Suganuma was the only person I'd met up with outside work too. Every single one of my childhood and college friends now had their own family, and for years now the only contact I had with them was liking each others' social media posts. I knew I shouldn't really have been meeting up with Suganuma either, but I kept making the excuse to myself that she was like family.

"I was really lonely. Intensely lonely. It was like it was seeping into my bones," she went on. "The other day I happened to catch a documentary on TV about unmarried siblings in their seventies living together. How nice, I thought, but I don't even have siblings. And then I remembered you, Hirai."

"Ah."

"I'm not interested in getting married, but of course I can't say the same for you. Like I said, if you ever do get a boyfriend you can leave any time. In that case I'll just give up and go back to living in a tiny studio flat."

Having apparently said what she wanted, she picked up her beer glass and downed what was left of it. Staring into the bottom of the glass, in a light tone she said once more, "So how about it? Will you live with me?"

I couldn't answer.

"Go home and think it over. But let me know as soon as you can, okay?"

"Okay, I will. I know you're serious. But don't get your hopes up too much," I just about managed to say, and she gave me a thin smile. Then she listened to me moan about my job until I'd finished my lemon sour.

It wasn't normal, I thought. Suganuma couldn't care less about whether something was normal or not. For a time she'd even casually worn a plastic ring she'd made on her 3D printer on the third finger of her left hand.

But I was scared of choosing something so out of the ordinary. I found it easier to be as plain and unobtrusive as possible, which suited my personality and appearance.

Still, this option of doing something out of the ordinary was growing on me by the day. Even so, I couldn't bring myself to do it, and it was only after autumn had passed and we were deep into winter that I finally made up my mind.

I didn't get much sunlight in my apartment, and it was freezing cold. Even when I ramped up the heating to the highest setting, I still felt the need to wear a down jacket. One particularly cold day in February, I was huddled in bed. Some time had passed since my bath, and my hands and feet were already feeling cold again. I rubbed my hands together under the covers and held them between my thighs, but they still wouldn't warm up. As I curled up and waited for my bed to get warm, memories of the past ran through my mind. The winter I'd spent with my mother and grandmother in the penetrating cold of the housing estate. The stink of the kerosene heater. The jewel-like chocolates from Wako in Ginza that my grandmother bought for us as a special treat only at New Year. How the dust dancing in the back of the kitchen sparkled. How we'd been much poorer than I was today, but we'd never really felt our poverty in the bustle of daily life.

When I opened my eyelids, the familiar ceiling was tranquil and submerged in darkness. Loneliness seeped into my bones. Huddled up under the covers, I was reminded quite naturally of what Suganuma had said.

"Am I too late?"

When I called Suganuma to let her know, I was a bit taken aback by her delighted response. It sounded like she was jumping for joy on the other end of the line. She lost no time in finding us a flat, and with startling efficiency exchanged contracts and set a date for the move. It happened so fast I couldn't help thinking that if she only handled her work in the same way she'd be able to live in a larger flat of her own.

Having seemingly given up on getting somewhere central, she chose a second-floor condo a ten-minute walk from Tsurumi Station in Yokohama, a sunny 2LDK with separate toilet and bathroom that I could never have afforded on my salary alone.

I ended up having to ask her to delay the move by a month after I forgot to arrange for the disposal of large items from my current place that I would no longer need. I'd assumed the removals company would deal with it all, but it seemed that kind of service didn't exist. I'd also been intimidated by web pages stating forcefully, "You must never transport items you intend to throw away to your new residence."

Had that really been four months ago already? I went through the automatic door into the convenience store with the memory of Suganuma's pushiness still going around my mind.

I walked around the store and finally found the photocopier in the third corner. Following the instructions on the touch panel, I took out a USB memory stick from my bag and inserted it into the machine, then selected a PDF file and pressed start.

It began noisily printing the file, ejecting copy paper from the cavity at its centre. I picked it up, still warm, inserted it into a clear plastic file, and put it in my bag.

I would have preferred a pack of six toilet paper rolls, but convenience stores only sold packs of four. I picked up one in plain packaging, apparently the store's own brand.

When I opened the door to our flat, Suganuma was in the living room. "I'm home!" I called as I removed my pumps.

"Hi there," she said, turning to me. "Oh great, toilet paper!"

I put the pack down outside the bathroom door and went into my bedroom.

My room was quite small, barely six tatami mats in size. It had already felt claustrophobic with just a bed and storage drawers, and I'd had to squeeze in a desk too for the brief time that working from home had been introduced, and that had made it hopelessly cramped. It felt smaller than it actually was, and I pretty much only ever used it for sleeping in.

I took the clear plastic file out of my bag, and after a moment's hesitation I hid it away in a desk drawer.

Whenever I stepped into the living room, I breathed a sigh of relief at the air that wrapped around my body. We had only the bare minimum of furniture there, with a low table, two-seater sofa, and the TV and stand, the 3D printer looking out of place in the corner. Suganuma was sitting on the sofa fiddling with her smartphone.

I put the cans of beer and chuhai I'd brought home from work down on the table in front of her.

"Here you go."

She instantly looked up. "Eh? What's the occasion?" she asked, staring at the shiny silver cans.

"Leftovers from the drinks party at work."

"Nice! Okay, I'll make dinner then."

She got up and went to the kitchen, where she started opening and closing the fridge and pressing buttons on the microwave. Steam rose as she lifted the lid off a saucepan, and I could smell something like consommé. After a while, she served up stuffed cabbage rolls, potato salad, and white rice on the living-room table.

We sat on floor cushions by the table and briefly put our hands together in thanks for the meal. The cabbage rolls were piled up on a round white plate I'd bought at the hundred-yen shop. I took a bite of one, and the sweet cabbage melted in my mouth.

"It's delicious," I told her. "Making cabbage rolls is so fiddly."

Suganuma nodded as she broke one up with her chopsticks. The way she held her chopsticks, with them sticking out of her clenched fist, was unusual. I'd initially been surprised at how well she could pick things up like that.

"It's not that much trouble when you get used to it."

As I enjoyed the meal, warmth spread through the core of my body. What I'd seen at work today flashed through my mind, and so I told Suganuma about it as she quietly chewed on her food.

"You know what? The old guy who sits opposite me was wearing a polo shirt, and it had a design on the chest that however I thought about it looked like the outline of a prefecture."

"A prefecture?" Suganuma tilted her head, uncomprehending.

"I meant to look it up," I said, reaching for my phone. I input "map of Japan" into the search bar, and found a map where the borders between prefectures were clearly outlined. I zoomed in on it, starting from the north. As I gradually moved down the map, suddenly my hand stopped.

"Got it! It's Wakayama!"

Suganuma burst out laughing. "A polo shirt with Wakayama on it? What the hell is that?"

"It's weird, but that's what he was wearing. I wonder if he'll wear it again on Monday. I want to check if I got it right."

"He'll probably be wearing Nara on Monday!"

I laughed too. "That's hilarious!"

Suganuma lifted up her plate and drank the remaining soup from the cabbage rolls, then briskly cleaned up her own dishes and went to run the bath. I listened to it running as I chewed on the sweet cabbage.

I got out of the bath to find Suganuma pushing the sofa back against the wall, shifting it bit by bit.

"What are you doing?"

"Tomorrow's a holiday. I've already sent off the dog figurines and I just finished designing a system screen for work, so today I'm going to watch videos in the living room until I fall asleep."

Once the sofa was finally flush against the wall, she turned and looked directly at me with her flat-lidded almond-shaped eyes.

"You gonna join me and sleep in here, Hirai?"

"Maybe I will."

"Yay!"

She went back into her room, and reemerged with a rolled-up semi-double mattress. Stood on its side, it came up to her chin, and when she laid it out in the seven-mat living room it covered practically the whole floor.

She put out some pillows and a terry cloth blanket, then inserted a DVD into the PS2 with a practised hand. She had brought the PS2 she used as a DVD player from her previous place. It was showing its age and would often skip bits. The only light in the darkened room came from the 32-inch TV screen. I sat on the mattress and watched.

"I'll have another beer!" Suganuma said, going to the fridge in high spirits.

The TV was showing a darkened stage. Suddenly it was flooded with light and sound, and cheers rose from the audience. The back of the stage rose slowly, gradually revealing Igarashi-kun and Kobachi dressed all in white. Once the stage was fully up, there was a moment of silence. Neither of them made the slightest movement. The audience held their breath and gazed at them. One of their old hits started playing, and Igarashi-kun and Kobachi burst into smiles and started dancing. Once again the audience roared. The camera panned out to show a bird's-eye view of the stage and the audience packed tightly in the auditorium, waving glow sticks and fans, swaying like a single living creature.

Three years ago, Suganuma and I had both been part of that swaying creature, frantically waving our glow sticks. Suganuma was a huge fan of the duo's pop group KI Dash and had all their DVDs. I was not as crazy about them as she was, but whenever I watched the concert we'd gone to, all the wild enthusiasm of that night came back to me, so I liked putting it on now and then.

"I always think Igarashi-kun's dancing here is great," Suganuma said. "He never slows down!" She had quietly joined me on the mattress, sitting cross-legged and sipping on her beer.

"Yeah," I agreed, feeling proud for some reason. "He trains really hard."

Suganuma was into Kobachi, while I was an Igarashi-kun fan. Igarashi-kun's athleticism was unbelievable for someone over forty, and the audience couldn't take their eyes off him. I was always impressed by his complex footwork, which was not only fast but smooth too. Nowadays idols were expected to be great dancers, but that wasn't the case twenty years ago, when KI Dash were at their peak. Since then, though, there had been a glut of boy bands, and they all started to hone their dance and vocal skills to distinguish themselves from the others and those skills had escalated. I loved how seriously Igarashi-kun took his art, even now that he had a solid fan base, putting on an overwhelming performance and not only keeping up with his younger rivals but outdoing them. I always went on about things like this to Suganuma when I got drunk, and resolved to keep it to myself today.

For a while I was absorbed in watching the DVD, but suddenly I was overcome with sleepiness. Unable to keep my eyes open, I snuggled down under the blanket and lay my head on the pillow.

Suganuma turned the volume down as I started slipping into a pleasant sleep. The sixth track was playing. I liked the way Igarashi-kun looked when he changed into a more casual outfit after this song. His figure was getting blurred and fuzzy. Someone was congratulating me. Kondo-san. No, it was my mother. My mother, who looked thinner and smaller every time I saw her. Sawako, are you living with someone? I never knew you had anyone like that. When are you getting married? No, no, it's not like that. Don't get your hopes up!

As far as I was concerned, my decision to move in with Suganuma meant that I'd given up. A future in which I was married and had children was looking impossible. Thirty-eight should still be too early to give up hope, but I just felt everything would be so much easier if I stopped trying. That was all. So no, Mum, don't get your hopes up.

In my life up to now, I had never once felt attracted to a man.

I had dated two guys, one in university and one when I had already been working three years. I hadn't completely disliked either of them, my feelings just never went beyond not disliking them. Even holding hands led to an uncomfortable feeling welling up in me that was hard to ignore, and having sweet nothings whispered into my ear was a real turn-off.

When I was thirty, I went to a matchmaking party to test whether there was really no hope for me. I decided to contact one of the men from it, and we'd gone out to dinner several times. I couldn't even remember what he was like now. I'd already felt suffocated when he invited me back home with him. I said I wasn't feeling too well and beat a hasty exit.

So I couldn't envision a future in which I would get married or have kids. Suganuma would have said that it was okay that way, wasn't it? and laughed it off.

When I woke up it was past noon and Suganuma was gone. I could hear the sound of the washing machine churning clothes. The sunshine pouring into the living room was so bright I wondered how it hadn't woken me up earlier. I must have kicked off the blanket in my sleep, as it was now bundled up by my feet. I picked up my phone and lay back lazily on the mattress. Just then the washing machine played a jaunty melody indicating the cycle had finished. Reluctantly I got up.

Hanging up the laundry was my job. Suganuma couldn't do it as she had a phobia of balconies. She'd told me that when she was in high school, her father had got angry with her for having the radio on too loud and shut her out on the balcony. She had spent three hours out there in the middle of winter just in her loungewear, and had ended up pissing herself.

The balcony was burning hot in the direct sunlight. I grimaced and shielded my eyes with one hand as I hung up the pieces of clothing one by one on the laundry pole.

I met Suganuma six years ago. At the time, the printing company where I worked had at long last decided to embark on a radical overhaul of the office-computer admin systems. After having obtained quotes from a number of companies, the work had been outsourced to CIE Tech, a systems firm whose sales pitches I often used to bin.

The initial "kick-off" meeting was attended by six men and women from CIE Tech. They all looked young and trendy, emanating what Mrs Kondo described as "an ultra-stylish aura". Suganuma had been among those six.

At their request, we provided three desks for them next to Accounts.

It was March and I was frantically busy with the accounts for the final quarter, so was the last left on my work island. Finally done with work for the day, I looked around and saw that the only other light still on was coming from the CIE Tech desks.

As the last one left, I did the standard check of the office, ticking off the items on the form provided. Once I'd finished, I went over to the CIE Tech desks near the exit clutching the form to my chest. The only one left that night was Suganuma. She was sitting hunched over her work in one corner of the almost completely dark office, her slim legs crossed, looking not so much serious as bored. Thinking that she seemed off guard and might be startled at the sound of my voice, I said cautiously, "Thanks for your hard work today. I'm off now. Please let the guard know when you leave."

She turned around and looked at me with her single-lidded eyes, not bothering to hide her boredom.

"Sure, will do. Have a good evening. I'm always the last, so I know what to do."

She turned back to her computer. I bowed, and was just on my way out when I realized that I'd forgotten to tick one of the items on the office check form.

"Oh, sorry, could I borrow a pen for a sec?"

Suganuma picked up the ballpoint pen on her desk and handed it to me. "Here you go."

I ticked the box for "Lock cabinets" and then automatically clicked the top of the pen, but the tip didn't retract. I tried again, but it only made a sound and vibrated slightly. Maybe it's the twist type, I thought, and tried turning it with both hands, but it didn't budge.

"Huh? That's weird..."

Suganuma saw me trying to twist the pen looking puzzled, and a faint smile played around her lips. "Oh, that. It's broken."

"Broken?"

She took the pen from my hands and, no longer smiling, gave a quick bow and said, "Have a good evening."

"Oh, thanks. You too. See you!"

That was the first conversation Suganuma and I had ever had, just the two of us. That was all it was, but for some reason the image of Suganuma bathed in the light of the computer screen with a wry smile on her face lingered at the back of my mind.

The next time we spoke was a week later. I was on my lunch break and headed to the local Doutor café, which was always busy at that hour. When I joined the queue of customers, mostly office workers from the neighbourhood by the look of them, I recognized the back of the woman in front of me. She was wearing a slim-fitting suit and staring at her phone, looking bored.

"Suganuma-san?"

She turned around in surprise, then her eyes softened. I'd intended to just make polite conversation, but then my gaze was drawn to her phone's screensaver. It showed Igarashi-kun and Kobachi facing each other, smiling.

"That's KI Dash, isn't it?" I blurted out, then felt flustered for having been so rude. "Oh, I'm sorry. I shouldn't have been looking at your phone."

"No worries," she said with a smile, shaking her head. "Do you like them too?"

"Yes. They're my generation."

"Hah. Which one do you like?"

"Igarashi-kun."

"I'm a Kobachi groupie."

We grinned at each other. The queue at Doutor was moving slowly, the server holding up her hand, a fixed smile on her face as she called out, "Over here, please!"

"So it wasn't snap, then," I said with a smile.

"If it was, I guess we'd be rivals. Have you been to any of their concerts?"

"Yeah, but that was like over ten years ago."

"No way! You should definitely go again. They're the best live."

Just as she was getting fired up, Suganuma reached the head of the queue and went on up to the counter to place her order. Realizing I still had a big smile on my face, I pulled the corners of my mouth back down and stared at her profile as she pointed at the menu.

After I'd placed my order and turned around holding my Milano Sandwich B, I saw that she was waiting for me as if it were the natural thing to do.

A year later, after two trial runs, the system that CIE Tech had built finally went live. The desks assigned to the workers were removed, and the day came when the CIE Tech employees were leaving for good. That day two emails from Suganuma arrived at my work email address. One was addressed to all the project members, a standard message of thanks for the year's work. The other one was to me alone.

Dear Hirai-san

How about going out for a drink outside work sometime? Here are my private contact details, so please do get in touch.

090-xxxx-xxxx

A month passed before I finally resolved to call her. After that we went out drinking once a month. We became friends and went to concerts together, and after a few years we dropped the "san" when calling each other by name.

When we'd spoken so passionately about KI Dash in Doutor that time, and even on the occasions when I was drunk and stayed over in her apartment, it had never occurred to me that we might end up living together. One night, not long after we'd moved in, Suganuma opened her heart to me. We'd gone out to eat at a local Chinese restaurant and, egged on by the friendly waiter, she had drunk too much Shaoxing wine and her face was flushed red.

"I'll never get married, not ever. If I ever started living with a guy on the condition that we'd never get married, I still might get pregnant, or his feelings might change. And then I'd be in deep shit. I don't want to take that risk."

"But you used to have a boyfriend, didn't you? A couple of years ago?"

"Having a boyfriend is different from getting married. That's what my mother always said about my father—he was so nice when they were just dating." Still holding on to some cha tsai pickles at one end of the dish with her chopsticks, she went on, "Once you're an adult, you can't choose the people around you, can you? Not your parents or siblings, obviously, but not the colleagues you generally interact with either, nor your team members. You don't get to choose them because you like them."

"I guess."

"I'm over forty now, and I can live my life without causing trouble for anyone else." With a tight smile, she put the cha tsai in her mouth and chewed on it. "If I can have my own way, I choose to be with you, Hirai, because I like you."

Embarrassed, I couldn't respond. I gulped down my oolong tea, now diluted by melted ice. The following day, Suganuma had forgotten the entire conversation.

A cold touch on my hand brought me back to myself. I slowly passed a coat hanger through Suganuma's wet T-shirt. She had been wearing it for several years already, and the neckline was getting stretched. By the time I finished hanging the washing out, I could feel sweat trickling down my back. The glass door rattled as I opened it. I picked up the laundry basket and was about to step through the door frame when I froze. Suganuma was standing in the living room with her legs apart and arms crossed. The blood had drained from her face, and she was staring at me.

"What's wrong?" I put down the laundry basket and rushed over to her.

"It's Kobachi..."

"What? Has there been a scandal or something?"

She shook her head. Her long hair rippled as it spread out from side to side.

"An accident? He's sick?"

She shook her head again.

"He... got married?"

She nodded. "A shotgun wedding," she managed to say in a voice that sounded like it came from the bowels of the earth.

"Who to?"

"A glamour model fifteen years younger than him."

As her words sank in, I looked up at the ceiling. The sun streaming in from the balcony was burning my back.

"Suganuma, are you okay?"

"I don't know." She shook her head, her face ghostly white as she stood rooted to the spot gripping her phone in one hand.

"Shall I make some lunch?"

I went to the kitchen and opened the fridge. Some noodles for yakisoba caught my eye. I took out some bacon and cabbage and put them on the small countertop. Glancing into the living room, I saw Suganuma sitting motionless on the sofa. I took out my phone and stealthily googled "Kobachi wedding". Instantly thumbnail photos of Kobachi and his wife came up. I tapped on the first article and enlarged the photo of the woman. White cleavage protruded from her low-cut T-shirt. Her slightly drooping eyes were fringed by thick eyelashes, her plump lips partly open. I quietly turned the screen off. It seemed like womanhood had been condensed into this one photo. It was enough to give me heartburn.

Suganuma was more heartbroken than I'd imagined. I thought she was being a bit over the top, but then I couldn't say what kind of feelings would be appropriate when an idol you'd been obsessively following for over twenty years married a glamour model fifteen years his junior after getting her pregnant.

She hardly touched the yakisoba I'd made. She spent the whole day sitting on the sofa without eating or drinking. Now and then, as if remembering, she picked up her phone, but immediately threw it down again. Outside the window, the sky turned briefly red and finally the dark of night arrived.

"What do you want for dinner? I'm thinking of getting something delivered."

I opened a food delivery app on my phone and tapped on several recommended restaurants. A photo of fried chicken jumped out at me, and I felt a pang of hunger as though my brain had been stimulated.

"Whatever." Sitting on the sofa, she shook her head.

"How about some udon? Will you eat it if I get some?"

She didn't answer, and just slowly slumped down on the sofa. I couldn't see her expression as she lay there with her hair spread around her face, her skinny shoulders poking up.

"Hirai, take me somewhere far away..."

I knew how much Suganuma loved Kobachi. Even if he was an icon from a distant world, she couldn't separate the real Kobachi who had chosen marriage in his private life from the idol Kobachi she was so obsessively devoted to. Wasn't there some way I could help to soothe her broken heart, even just a little? How far away could I take her?

"What about Atami?" I said, naming the first place that came to mind.

Suganuma didn't so much as twitch. I was so taken aback by what I'd just said that it took a few moments for my brain to get into gear and catch up with me.

"Let's go there on a day trip tomorrow. We can eat some seafood. And go to an onsen."

I looked at the phone in my hand and opened the travel app. It was an hour and a half from Tsurumi to Atami on regular train lines. Not an impossible distance for a day trip.

"Or shall we stay there overnight? We could always skive off work on Monday."

As I kept talking, Suganuma finally sat up. Her long hair had fallen forward over her face and she stared up at me through it.

"Do you mean it?"

I nodded.

The Green Car on the Tokaido Line was a double decker with low ceilings. We took inconspicuous seats at the back of the bottom deck. It was a Sunday morning train headed out of Tokyo, and not all that crowded. Other than us, there were only a few young people out on dates and elderly married couples. Gazing out of the window at the area around Totsuka Station, it wasn't so different from Tsurumi. A ginormous shopping mall flashed by.

Suganuma was sitting next to me sucking on a sweet. Compared to last night, she looked a lot more relaxed now. This morning she had even gobbled up two of the bread rolls I'd got from the convenience store.

"How long since you last went to Atami?" she asked at last, gazing out of the window.

"I went on my own in year three of middle school."

She looked at me, tilting her head questioningly. "That's a bit young to be going alone, isn't it?"

"Yep. I ran away from home."

"Wow. That must have taken some guts."

Now and then I caught a whiff of the candy she was sucking on. I was relieved that she was able to hold a proper conversation with me, so I dredged up some of my memories from the past.

"It was right after Masatoshi moved in with us."

Masatoshi was my second father, who moved in with us when I was fifteen. I say my second father, but it's not like I knew the first one. He'd already left by the time I was old enough to understand what was going on around me.

"So you stayed in a hotel there?"

"No, I didn't have enough money for that. When night fell, I got scared and went into an onsen hotel. I was hanging around the corner in the lobby where they sell souvenirs and a member of staff asked me, You haven't run away, have you?"

It had only been then that I realized what I'd done.

"I said I had."

"That was pretty honest of you."

I recalled how shaky my voice had been, and how I'd immediately burst into tears after answering them.

"I'd just stormed out of the house without any kind of plan. I also meekly gave them the phone number for home, and my mother came to pick me up."

I'd sat motionless in the hotel's office until there were two impatient knocks on the heavy steel door. The moment my mother opened it and saw me there, her taut face distorted as though she was about to cry, before immediately stiffening again.

"Well, if you ever run away from home again, Hirai, I'll know where to come look for you!" Suganuma said.

She laughed brightly, and I laughed with her. The train slowed as it entered a station and came to a halt, and several people got onto the Green Car we were in.

"The next stop after Ofuna is Fujisawa, right?" Suganuma asked as she gazed at the station, her tone unchanged from a moment ago.

"I want to see the sea," Suganuma said after we'd got off the train and were standing in Atami Station.

I looked at my phone and pointed towards the shopping arcade. "The inn is by the sea. Let's go and have lunch around there."

The area around Atami Station hadn't changed much. There was a surprising number of young people, and it was brimming with the vibrancy typical of a tourist resort. The shops in the arcade were blatantly aimed at tourists, greeting us with their fake Japanesey appearance. I gazed nostalgically at the white steam rising from the onsen-steamed manju buns displayed ostentatiously at the front of one shop.

We walked a little way and stopped outside a soba restaurant that didn't have a queue outside. I hesitated, unable to see inside the restaurant from the street, but Suganuma went ahead and opened the door. Instantly I felt the blast of artificial cold air from the air conditioner, and became aware of how sweaty my body was.

The building gave the impression of being old, with its exposed beams made from thick tree trunks. The interior was bigger than I'd thought, and it was bustling with a range of customers from youngsters to local senior residents. A little old woman came out from the back of the restaurant, glanced at us, and pointed at a nearby table. A sigh of relief escaped me as I sat down, even though we hadn't walked far.

I ordered soba noodles with grated yam, while Suganuma chose soba noodles with tempura. Her large serving of tempura came piled up on a rectangular dish. Watching her steadily work her way through the mound starting from the left, I was relieved to see that her appetite had returned.

The soba and grated yam slipped easily down my throat. I didn't know much about the different types of soba, so I was just satisfied that its taste and texture were how I'd imagined they should be.

"I mean," Suganuma started, as she dipped her noodles in the sauce, "if Kobachi had married someone around thirty-eight, maybe not such a great beauty, an actress or singer with real presence and talent, say, I could have dealt with that." She noisily slurped up some noodles and immediately went on, "I want her to have skills. If she really had substance, I'd have to admit defeat."

I mentioned the name of an actress that came to mind, and she pulled a face.

"What about an ordinary woman, then?"

"No. That would be too much like me."

"I wonder where that sort of feeling comes from," I said, then realizing this sounded a bit cold, I hastily added, "but I get why you hate that she's a glamour model, seriously."

"I mean, it's not like he even had to announce it. Celebrities never announce things like moving house, or a parent dying or whatever, so why do they make a big thing about getting married and having babies? It's all part of their private life. It's fine to keep all of that a mystery."

I neither agreed nor disagreed, just kept slurping my noodles.

The light outside was blinding as we left the restaurant. The roof of the arcade was transparent, and the sunlight shone mercilessly through it.

On one side of the street, a couple was taking a selfie of themselves holding onsen manju buns. The boy was tall and thin, the hair on the back of his small head closely cropped. Kids these days must find this sort of onsen town novel and interesting.

Atami still retained some of its Showa period aura, and only the people on the streets kept changing. Seeing Suganuma looking goggle-eyed at the surroundings, the back of my fifteen-year-old self running away to Atami twenty-four years ago flashed through my mind.

"You know what? I ran away three times between the ages of fifteen and seventeen."

"Seriously, Hirai? And there I was thinking you were such a good girl."

"In year two of high school, I thought that if I could just get into university I'd be able to live on my own. Once I had that aim in mind, I settled down."

"Did you hate home that much?"

"Yeah, well, it was because of Masatoshi. I mean, he was a really good person, but I just couldn't get my head around living with this middle-aged man who'd suddenly come into our life."

"I guess it was just when you were going through adolescence too."

As we emerged from the arcade, a road going up a steep slope came into view. Even here there were restaurants and bars aimed at tourists. There was a newish-looking place selling sweets that looked to me like they were just strawberries with skewers through them, unsurprisingly with young people queueing up outside. I'd cooled down in the air conditioning of the restaurant, but walking in the street my body was soon covered in sweat again.

"I liked it better before Mum married Masatoshi, when we lived with my grandmother, just the three of us in the danchi. We were poor, and there was even a time I was always late with my school lunch money."

Life in the danchi, always waiting in our dirty, cramped apartment for my super busy mother, was now a warm memory embedded in my heart. On the other hand, memories of living in Masatoshi's smart flat were blurred, and I had to work hard to retrieve them.

I realized that I was talking about myself too much, too shackled to the vision of that girl's back.

"Didn't you ever run away from home, Suganuma?"

Suganuma shook her head emphatically. "I was far too scared of what would happen if I did something like that. I could never have done it unless I was determined never to go back home."

"Oh," I replied in a whisper so low that she probably didn't hear me. In the distance, I could see a short section of horizon peeping between the buildings.

We'd wanted to see the sea, but coming to the swimming beach had been a mistake. It was soon after the beach had opened for the season, and the sand was covered in beach parasols. Countless black heads bobbed over the surface of the water, packed in so closely that they looked as though they would crack against each other. The relentlessly shrill voices of children billowed back and forth over the incessant sound of the waves.

The sunlight became ever stronger the closer we got to the sea, and our T-shirts began sticking to our backs. We stood at the entrance to the swimming beach, lost for words.

"Wow."

"Seriously?" Suganuma shifted her bag onto her other shoulder and muttered, "I'd imagined Atami was much more run down than this."

"Maybe it's because they haven't been able to come to the beach for a few years due to the pandemic?"

I looked around and saw there were several beach huts with banners hanging up outside. One with "soft cream" written in white letters on a sky-blue background caught my eye.

"Ice cream..." I murmured.

Suganuma wiped her forehead with a handkerchief and nodded. "Yes, let's go and get some."

We stepped onto the sand and headed for the sky-blue banner, threading our way through children running around and groups of young men and women. Sand got into my sneakers with each step and they started filling up. The beach was overflowing with flesh of all kinds. Girls with white skin and delicate bodies stretched out beside lean tanned men. Three young women walking towards us were all about the same height and wore similar makeup, but they were each of a different build. The one in the middle was the thinnest, with few curves. The six legs extending from their swimwear wiggled rawly, and I reflexively averted my eyes. I looked down and stared at my grubby sneakers sinking into the sand.

Suganuma suddenly stopped ahead of me. "Hirai, what flavour?"

I looked up to see we had reached the beach hut with the banner. Several people were queueing up on the wooden deck outside the building.

"Vanilla."

"I'll get them."

Without hesitating, Suganuma joined the queue of swimsuit-clad people. The collar of her short-sleeved blouse fluttered as she pulled out her purse.

She came back carrying brown and white ice creams and held the white one out to me. I thanked her and carefully took it from her.

"Is it okay if we sit here?" Suganuma asked a member of staff passing behind us, pointing at the wooden steps to the deck. The guy had blonde hair and I was startled to see he had a tattoo on his sun-tanned left arm.

"Go for it," he responded somewhat flippantly.

Suganuma gave a light bow, and we squeezed ourselves into the shade on the steps.

I bit off a chunk of the ice cream with my lips, and it instantly turned to liquid in my mouth with no resistance. After I'd taken two mouthfuls from one side, the other side was already dripping. I held it away from my body while frantically taking bites. Several white spots appeared on the wood deck.

We ate our ice creams in silence, and by the time I'd finished mine my hands were all sticky. As the cold settled in my stomach, I could feel my body cooling down a bit. I caught my breath and said to Suganuma, "It looks like there's a park over there. Could be more relaxing there."

"It's all right. I'm getting the seaside vibe right here."

Chewing on the cone, she shook her hand to dislodge some bits of ice cream stuck to it.

Before us, everything was blue. Closer to the horizon, the blue of the sky took on a whitish tinge while the blue of the sea darkened. Every time the surface of the sea swelled up, squeals of joy rose from the people floating in it. Irrespective of the human reaction, the relentless sound of the surging waves continued to engulf the entire beach.

Feeling my body heating up again, I couldn't quite find the energy to stand up.

The room I had reserved was in a large ryokan clearly dating back to the Showa period. The exterior walls had probably once been white but were now grubby and dark. We went through the automatic doors in silence, and I was relieved to see that the interior was clean, so it must have been renovated. In the huge, carpeted lobby, a child was running around beside a young couple dressed in yukata and carrying a change of clothes on their way back from the bath. The floorplan I had been given while checking in showed they had somehow managed to squeeze in everything from a banqueting hall to a karaoke room, bar, table tennis room, games corner and large communal bathing areas.

After dinner, we changed into yukata and headed for the baths. Strangely, the sight of so many naked women in the bathing area didn't seem as raw as the exposed flesh on the beach, maybe because the age bracket was higher. The effect of gravity on the flabby bodies of some middle-aged women sitting on the edge of the bath made itself felt in their slackly hanging breasts.

Suganuma's naked body was skinny. Her ribs stood out in sharp relief, and the bumpy form of her spine was exposed. Her breasts were determinedly flat. Year by year my own lower body was getting bulkier as it stored up excess fat, and I kept it covered with my wash towel.

After our bath, we decided to go to the bar in the basement of the ryokan. We opened the heavy wooden door and saw that nobody else was in there. It was a small space with only a few seats at the wooden counter, and three tables with red sofas. Jazz was playing at low volume. For a while we were left standing in the doorway wondering what to do before a man with a bow tie poked his head out and hastily gestured for us to sit at the counter.

Countless whisky bottles were lined up on the walls. It had a retro theme, with stained-glass lamps and black rotary-dial telephones placed here and there.

I ordered a Manhattan from the cocktail menu. Suganuma flicked back and forth through the pages of the menu several times, then requested some sort of whisky on the rocks.

I glanced around at details in the bar while we waited for our drinks, and Suganuma took out her phone. On the screen glowing in the dim bar was a photo of the woman Kobachi had married. Startled, I said without thinking, "You putting a curse on them or something?"

Suganuma shook her head, the yukata she'd hastily thrown on falling open with the movement.

"No, I'm just searing it into my memory."

"Best not do that. It's bad for your health."

Her serious profile carried on staring at the face of the woman who looked far rawer than anyone I'd seen today.

"Why did he choose her? Why can't I see her in a positive light?"

"I don't think many women would be able to see her in a positive light," I answered, gazing at the photo of the woman showing her cleavage and smiling broadly.

"I hate that this is who he married, and I hate that he chose to get married to begin with," she spat. "I've got to get over this feeling of disgust somehow."

A glass of whisky was quietly placed in front of her. The cubes of ice in it tinkled faintly.

"I never got round to asking you this, Hirai, but do you want to get married?"

I felt the blood drain from my face at this sudden question, and smiled vaguely.

"I really don't know."

Now it was my turn to have a Manhattan in a tall cocktail glass placed in front of me. Staring at the rim of the glass, I cautiously attempted to coax out the words in my heart.

"I'm the sort of person who can't fall in love," I said. "And I didn't want my mother to remarry. I just can't identify with the value that marriage equals something good, so I'm probably just like you, Suganuma."

The Manhattan's heavy alcoholic aroma contrasted with its sweet-looking deep red colour.

"But then, sometimes I feel that I'm being childish for wishing my mother hadn't remarried, even after so many years."

I could feel my cheeks growing hot as I drank.

"If I never get married or give birth, maybe I'll never get to grow up. So sometimes I think I should probably get married after all."

"Yeah, that resonates with me. I also think I'm really kiddy sometimes."

There was a clanging noise as the door to the bar

was pushed open. I glanced over and saw a man dressed in a yukata standing there alone.

"Irasshaimase. Please take a seat wherever you like."

The man sat at the counter to my left, leaving one seat between us. He picked up a menu and with a practised air ordered a whisky.

"Thank you, Hirai."

"What?" I hastily took my eyes off the man and looked at Suganuma's profile.

"If Igarashi-kun gets married, I'll bring you here too."

I laughed and nodded. "Yes, please do that."

"But I'll still be Kobachi's fan. I can't help it."

"Hey, are you talking about Kobachi from KI Dash?" the man sitting on my left interjected. I turned automatically to look at him and immediately fixated on the big nose enshrined at the centre of his face.

"Oh, sorry for butting in. I just heard about his marriage. Quite a shock, isn't it?"

My mind went blank. The man gave off a stale smell of alcohol, so he must have already been drinking. His skin was dark, and when I looked closer I could see several small pockmarks on his cheeks. He looked like he was in his late forties or so. The edges of his droopy eyes were carved with wrinkles so deep that dust could settle in them.

"You from Tokyo?"

Not knowing how to respond, I gave an involuntary nod. But strictly speaking I was from Kanagawa, I thought meaninglessly. My heart started beating hard, and my face grew hot.

"Really? Me too."

The man leaned forward, bringing his face so close I could almost feel his breath. I nearly caught a glimpse of bare skin through a gap in his yukata and averted my eyes. My pounding heartbeat echoed through my upper body.

"C'mon, what are you so scared of?"

"Excuse me, we're here on a trip to heal my broken heart," Suganuma piped up cheerfully from my other side. "Please leave us alone."

The man glanced at her and then, with a bored look, turned away from us.

"Oh well, if you change your mind just say so," he said, taking out his phone.

I turned to face Suganuma so that he was out of my vision. My heart was still racing.

"Shall we get something to munch on?" Suganuma asked, flicking through the menu.

But I couldn't think straight and just shook my head. "I'm going to the toilet."

I stood up and looked around the dark interior, and saw a door at the far end. I headed over to it, slippers flapping, and pushed it open.

Reflected in the mirror over the washbasin was a pale woman of medium build. The utterly nondescript face of a woman just shy of forty.

The man's grinning face flashed through my mind, and I clutched my chest. Those glittering eyes against withered skin. Had he been eyeing me up?

Gross. I clutched hold of the washbasin and closed my eyes. I took a few deep breaths and waited for my heartbeat to settle.

When I came out of the bathroom, the counter seats were immediately in front of me. The man was again leaning over and talking with Suganuma. I strode back over and pulled my seat out, glaring at him. He visibly flinched and moved away.

Suganuma picked up her empty glass and gave it a light shake.

"Finished. That wasn't bad."

"Huh?"

"Let's go. Thanks for indulging me."

"No problem," I said, shaking my head.

For some reason I felt like crying.

The next morning we woke up just before we were due to be at work. The sun was shining through the curtains, and I crawled out of my futon to open them. The undulating surface of the sea was bathed in the morning light, sparkling like a miracle.

We took turns shutting ourselves up in the bathroom to block out the sound of the ocean while we called our respective workplaces. I said that I'd come down with a fever, while Suganuma said she'd got stomach ache and felt nauseous.

We took a walk on the beach before the whole town got up, bought two cinnamon rolls on impulse at a bakery by the station, ate some seafood sashimi on rice, then went home. We took regular seats on the train this time to save money. The closer we came to Tokyo, the more people we saw dressed for work.

*

I went to stuff the large white envelope into the post box. As it was about to slip out of my fingers under its own weight, I involuntarily tightened my grip on it. I remained there for some moments, unable to move my hand.

I came to myself when I heard someone laugh nearby. I quickly chucked the envelope into my bag and started walking. As I stepped over the asphalt in my pumps, I tried as hard as I could to empty my head of thoughts.

When I opened the door to the flat, Suganuma was there in the hallway, frantically packing dog figurines into a cardboard box.

"Why won't they fit, dammit!"

She always got a lot of orders around the time of the Obon festival, when the souls of the departed return to earth, and for the last week had been spending all her time moving between the 3D printer and her computer.

The box was stuffed full of plain colourless figurines of dogs, each individually wrapped in a plastic bag, and several others lay scattered around the box as she tried to make them all fit. The painting process was apparently awaiting them at the box's shipping destination.

"Didn't you pack them alternately?" I took off my pumps and squeezed past her.

"Alternately?" she parroted, confused.

Clearly she wasn't thinking properly, and was just trying to force the remaining figurines into the already-full box.

"Like placing the feet and heads alternately." I gave up and knelt down next to her, showing her what I meant.

"Oh, like that!" she muttered weakly, and started removing all the figurines from the box.

Leaving her to it, I went into my room and put my bag down on the desk. Suganuma sometimes seemed to become a shell of herself when she was really busy. I doubted whether she would be able to cook dinner in this state. Maybe I should order a takeaway. I was about to head for the living room when my phone vibrated.

A phone call. I shut the door to my room again, looked at the screen and stiffened.

Mother, said the display. I stared at it for a while, but the vibrating showed no signs of stopping. The word Mother pulsed insistently along with the vibration. I tapped the screen with my index finger.

"Hello?"

"Sawako, is that you?"

It had been about three years since I'd last seen my mother. Bracing myself, I summoned a tone of voice as nonchalant as I could make it.

"Yep, hello there."

"Look, has your address changed? I sent you some sweets, but they were returned."

My heart started racing. I sat down on the bed, trying to pretend to my mother that nothing was up.

"Oh, er, yes... I've moved."

"You could at least have told me that much."

"I forgot. I'll send you the address."

"Has everything been okay?"

"Yeah, sure."

"We've got a dog now, you know."

"What?"

"He's so cute. Aki just showed me how to send photos, so I'll send you some."

Listening to her prattle away, it came back to me that, right, come to think of it, this was the way she spoke and that was what her voice sounded like, as though the gap in time were being filled in.

"Have you seen Aki?" I asked in spite of myself, feeling a rush of nostalgia at hearing her name. Aki was my cousin and two years younger than me.

"Yes. She's pregnant now. Apparently she had a really hard time of it with infertility treatment though."

"Really? Well that's good news then."

"And anyway, our dog's a shiba you know."

My mother's voice kept sounding in my ear, but little by little I stopped being able to understand the meaning of what she was saying. I stared at a corner of my desk, the irregular grain of the wood that was simply there.

My mother's voice droned on and on. I put in a few appropriate words here and there to show I was listening, although I wasn't sure I succeeded. But eventually, she seemed to be satisfied and hung up.

I tapped a folder on my phone titled "Stuff". A number of apps were grouped there. I opened one with a red logo on a white background.

For the first time in ages I looked at the login page and selected "Reauthorization". When I entered my email address and password, several notifications appeared in pop-ups.

<Congratulations! You have been matched with Ryo.>

<You have new likes.>

<A new feature has been added!>

As each new notification popped up, one after another, I methodically tapped to erase them. Photos of men appeared in a row at the top of the screen.

The doorbell rang and I heard Suganuma's footsteps rushing to answer it. As she passed the door to my room, I hastily turned off my phone screen. I heard the front door open, and then the voices of a man and Suganuma talking. It was probably the courier come to collect the dog figurines.

I turned my phone screen back on and opened the new messages page. Of six men, four had already withdrawn. I tapped on the first photo of the remaining two.

<Hello, nice to meet you! I'm happy to be matched with you. Looking forward to chatting!>

It was dated three weeks ago. The thumbnail photo showed a full body against an ocean backdrop, but it was too small for me to make out his face. Impulsively I typed in a reply.

<Hi! I haven't used the app for a while, sorry to have taken so long to reply. Happy to chat if you like.>

I pressed send without bothering to read over it again, then threw the phone down on the bed. I threw my body down on the bed too, and closed my eyes.

Fertility treatment. There had been no emotion whatsoever in my mother's voice as she'd uttered those words. She had never once pressed me about getting married or having children. The memory of lying with my thighs spread on the examination table and the feel of the white envelope came back to me. The words "maybe I can too" and "not a hope" jumbled together in my mind and surged behind my eyelids.

I let all the strength drain from my body. I gave myself over to gravity and sharpened all my awareness right up to my fingertips. I lay on the bed not moving an inch. Pretending to be dead. I sometimes did this.

I was dead. Nothing in this world had anything to do with me. I thought about the dead dogs. The dead dogs that had been doted on by their owners. They had left fake bodies in the world as figurines, and their souls were running around the other world wagging their tails. My soul joined them frolicking there.

I could hear Suganuma rummaging around in the living room. I stood up as though drawn by the sound.

She was in the middle of the room cutting up a large white sheet with a pair of scissors. Next to it lay a cardboard box. A piece of the sheet had been stuck onto one of its sides.

"What are you doing?"

With a big sweep of the scissors, the sea of white sheet parted in two. Thin threads hung from where she had cut it.

"I'm making a ritual burning corner."

Her tone of voice had returned to normal, so she must have felt more relaxed now the courier had collected the orders.

However, I didn't understand what she meant. Realizing that my silence meant I wanted her to explain, she continued without pausing her cutting, "The number of dud figurines are piling up, and I feel like if I just throw them away I'll be haunted by them."

"But it's not like you can keep them at home forever, is it?"

The pieces of sheet continued to get smaller and smaller under the scissors.

"Right. I looked on Amazon and found there's something called a ritual burning service. If you send them a box, they'll arrange to have it burned with full rites by a shrine or temple. In the meantime, I'll keep the duds in this. They say the ritual has more effect if you wrap the duds or just cover the box with white cloth."

"I never knew that sort of service existed!"

"Right? If you've got any old amulets or whatever, Hirai, feel free to put them in here."

"I'm surprised you're bothered by that sort of thing, Suganuma."

She laughed, and started spreading glue on a piece of sheet.

"Well, I'll admit to having thrown old amulets in the garbage, but I get a lot of letters and emails from dog owners thanking me for the figurines."

There were wrinkles in the sheet stuck on the side of the box, and one end was weirdly bulging out. Suganuma roughly folded the bulging part flat and glued it down.

"All those feelings for their dogs are really strong, and it gets a bit scary sometimes."

The finished box for ritual burning, patched up with bits of old sheet, looked like it had been made in an elementary school craft class. The rough finish, at odds with her words, was just like her, I thought.

"What do you want to do for dinner?"

Suganuma tilted her tousled head and thought a moment. "If you don't mind oyakodon, I'll make it right away."

"Really? That'd be great, thanks."

I sat down on the sofa and turned on the TV to a random channel. After a while, I heard Suganuma moving around in the kitchen. I listened intently to the sounds of her opening and closing the fridge and water hitting the sink, overlapping with the sound of someone laughing on TV.

*

I lay face down in bed and held my breath. I slowly closed my eyes, letting all the strength drain from my body. I was dead.

On my way home from work, I'd seen a woman with a pushchair. The baby in the pushchair couldn't have been one year old yet, and was asleep with its head slumped into its shoulders. The woman was wearing a short-sleeved dress with flat comfy shoes, and for a nursing mother looked very well groomed. Judging from her eyes and the veins on the back of her hand, though, she must have been in her forties. She had to be older than me.

It wasn't that unusual these days to have a baby in your forties. I knew that. But it didn't help. All the way home, a suffocating feeling clung to me as though I had swallowed something heavy.

When I got home, Suganuma wasn't there. She had messaged me saying she wouldn't be home tonight. I went straight to bed and stayed there over ten minutes pretending to be dead.

I imagined I was walking hand in hand with my grandmother on the far side of the river to the other world, and little by little the heavy feeling began to pass.

When I looked at the clock it was already after eight p.m. The four hours until bedtime felt absurdly long.

I put the fried chicken bento I'd bought at the convenience store into the microwave and pressed the start button. The bento started turning but immediately caught on the side of the microwave and stopped.

I stood there looking at my phone. I opened the app in my "Stuff" folder and found a message had arrived from the man.

<I went to Kamakura on the spur of the moment last week. Komachi-dori Street was packed, but luckily I managed to get a table in a restaurant and could take things easy. Have you been anywhere lately?>

I'd been corresponding with the man at the rate of a message every two days. This was the sixth message. I was about to start typing out a reply with my finger when the microwave pinged. I turned the phone screen off for the moment and took out the bento. One edge of the plastic container had warped with the heat.

I moved to the sofa and started typing out a reply while picking at the bento with disposable chopsticks.

Maybe I can, I thought. Even I was capable of exchanging messages with a man.

Time went by as it always did, even without Suganuma there, an ordinary night spent lying in bed in my room. The next morning, alone in utter silence in the living room, I opened a bag of six bread rolls.

I went to work, watered the ornamental plant—whatever it was—and sat down at my desk, then started in surprise.

Yoshida was sitting opposite me wearing his polo shirt. My gaze was sucked in by the embroidered motif on his chest. It was Wakayama Prefecture. It was the silhouette of Wakayama Prefecture I'd seared into my eyes, I was sure of it.

"Hirai-sensei, can I ask you something?"

I jumped at the sound of a voice behind me, and turned to see Mrs Kondo standing there, her head tilted enquiringly.

"Oh, I'm sorry to disturb you. I just wanted to check something with you."

"Yes?" I replied excessively briskly, trying to cover my surprise.

Mrs Kondo placed the document she was holding on to my desk, and I answered several questions she had about work.

After she had gone, I nonchalantly carried on looking at Yoshida's chest.

I wanted to tell Suganuma about it as soon as possible. I wanted to take a photo of it to send her, but of course I restrained myself.

A little after the regular time, I left the office. The peak of summer had passed, and once the sun had gone down it became a little cooler and there was a breeze. I felt chilly in my short-sleeved blouse and rubbed my arms, feeling left behind by the sudden change in season.

I dropped by the pharmacist at the nearest station and bought a six-pack of toilet roll. I hurried home, the bag of toilet paper hanging from my left hand swinging slightly. I wondered if Suganuma was already home.

When I opened the door to our home, the entrance and hallway were sunk in darkness and deathly quiet. I reached out my hand and turned on the light. The jumble of pumps and sandals in the small entrance way was unchanged since yesterday.

Maybe she was working overtime tonight? As I made my way to the living room I looked at my phone and saw that a message had come in from her.

<I probably won't be home tonight either. Sorry, but please go ahead and have dinner.>

"What the—?" I said aloud, sounding more wretched than I'd expected.

As I sat down on the sofa, I suddenly caught sight of the ritual burning corner. A quiet presence of death emanated from the white box. It was half full of figurines, some missing a leg or entwined with filament, others where I couldn't quite discern why they were judged to be duds.

Feeling at a loose end, I looked at my phone. I tapped on the "Stuff" folder, as I now did regularly. A reply to my last message had arrived. I would probably be invited out for a meal before long.

A message. I took a deep breath. Even I could send a message.

So should I meet him? Could I cope with meeting a man I didn't know, being exposed to his eyes evaluating me as a woman? For some reason Masatoshi's face started surfacing in the back of my mind, and I hastily opened the message.

<Me too, I often take it easy at home at weekends (ha ha!). By the way, I would love to meet you. Would you like to have lunch together one of these days? (^^)>

My heart skipped a beat. The image of Masatoshi's stiff smile the first time we met formed in my brain, although I tried to tell myself it was irrelevant. He was doing his best to smile behind his glasses, with his thinning hair and belly hanging over the top of his trousers. He was so unlike boys my own age, with sweat oozing from his greasy white skin however much he tried to wipe it away. It was bad enough that this was my new father, but I was utterly grossed out that my mother could fall in love with a man like this. Even so, I was dimly aware that it was also the choice of a single mother fed up with living in poverty. After she married Masatoshi, we moved to a comfortable apartment, she had a lot more time off, and I never got behind with my school lunch money again. Whatever the reason, though, it was the fact that my mother could ever have offered herself as a woman to Masatoshi that had weighed heavily on me ever since.

The man I was messaging now was only a bit younger than Masatoshi had been back then. Could I offer myself as a woman to him, just as my mother had done? Did I really want to do that?

My finger moved.

<Sure. I'd like to meet up too.>

I didn't want to. But, maybe I could. Maybe I was capable of it. The examination table partitioned off by a curtain came to mind. The unpleasant feeling of having my lower body exposed the other side of the curtain, and the sensation of the white envelope flashed up and disappeared again. Alone on the sofa in the dim light of the living room, I continued staring into the centre of myself.

*

The man introduced himself as Yuki Tanabe. He was of medium height and build, appropriate for someone aged forty. He turned up to the East Exit of Ikebukuro Station wearing a grey jacket over a white shirt, with a heavy-looking black bag slung over one shoulder. His body leaned slightly to the side as he walked. Shoulder bags always seemed excessively large on short men and it gave him an unsophisticated air. If he just changed his bag, he probably wouldn't be too bad, I thought. I was assessing him, I suddenly realized gloomily. He must be assessing me too. I didn't have any clothes suitable for a date, and this morning I'd stood staring at my wardrobe completely at a loss. The best I could come up with was a work blouse and bag paired with a dark blue flared skirt. I'd worn the skirt to work too until a few years ago, but then I'd thought it was a bit too young for the office and it had lain dormant inside the closet ever since. Seeing myself in the mirror wearing it now, I felt some vestiges of femininity left in me.

We went to the first suitable-looking restaurant near the station. A bell attached to the old-fashioned door rang as we entered. The place was tiny, and stuffed full of wine bottles and an assortment of plates and coffee mills and whatnot, but I couldn't tell whether they were meant to be stylish or if they'd just been put there out of convenience.

As soon as we sat down, Tanabe beamed at me. "I'm so happy you came today."

I didn't know how to respond, so I just smiled vaguely. He didn't seem at all put out by my reaction, and merely pointed at the menu and asked what I wanted to order.

I ordered the Pasta Set B, which consisted of a small amount of lettuce slapped onto a plate and a carbonara that was no different from what I made at home. At 1,080 yen, I couldn't help thinking that I could make it for less.

"Whereabouts do you live? I'm in Kashiwa."

"Tsurumi."

"Oh that's great, very convenient. Kashiwa's right over the other side of Tokyo. Our station is larger than you might expect. Have you ever been there?"

"Um, I don't think I ever got off at Kashiwa."

"Everyone who comes to my place is surprised by how much it's thriving. You have everything you need around the station area."

"Ah, I think I know what you mean."

"Have you always lived in the same area as now?"

"Yes, my family home is in Kanagawa too."

"How wonderful. A city girl, eh? I'm from Saga, in the back of beyond."

Tanabe sure did talk a lot. I never had to struggle to find something to say, for which I was grateful. He'd looked quiet at first, but actually he turned out to be cheerful and sociable. Over the next hour or so in the restaurant, we told each other pretty much everything about our daily lives. Except that I deliberately avoided mentioning that I lived with Suganuma. I still felt a lingering sense of guilt over living with another woman, like it was stuck to my back.

After the dishes had been cleared away and the waitress had stopped filling our empty glasses with water, Tanabe's smile got even bigger. The excessive visibility of his neat rows of small teeth had been bothering me for a while now whenever he smiled.

"Are you satisfied with your job?" he asked suddenly.

"What?" I stiffened slightly at the sudden change of subject.

"I have a side job, myself."

"Oh?"

"It involves helping to set up new businesses."

"Ah," I answered vaguely, not knowing what he was getting at.

Behind him, a couple of women who had come in some time after us were getting up and taking their money out to pay.

"For example, I think the way some people assume they have to stay in their job is such a waste. They're nipping their own potential in the bud. I want people like that to take on a challenge," he continued smoothly, as though reading from a script. "Surely there are things about your job you're not happy with, right, Hirai? You strike me as being a clever sort. Maybe your talent isn't appreciated, or you aren't able to put it to good use? Or the pay isn't good enough?"

"Oh no, I'm really not that great."

"You lack self-confidence, don't you? I was the same. But you should really use more positive language, you know. Do you know about kotodama?"

"Kotodama?"

"The spirit residing in words. If you imagine the sort of person you want to be, and keep saying that you want to be that person, and that you *will* be that person, eventually you will become them."

Well, I knew that. "Ah, okay."

Tanabe's eyes narrowed into crescent moons under his heavy eyelids.

"Do you read books?"

"Um, just a novel or whatever now and then. Do you like reading?" I asked quickly, relieved at the change in topic.

"I don't read novels," Tanabe answered flatly. "I believe it's crucial to read and absorb lots of books on self-improvement."

He suddenly took a book out of his big black shoulder bag and held it out to me. "Here, let me lend you this."

Printed large on the cover was a photo of foreign currency with the words, "Everything You Need to Know About Money Flow."

I shook my head, at a loss. "Um, no thanks."

"I'm sure it will be useful for you, Hirai. Please expand your possibilities," he said peremptorily, pushing the book towards me. The image of money sliding towards me over the table was terrifying. "There's someone I'd like to introduce you to," he went on. "If you don't mind, how about I bring them with me next time?"

"Someone else?" I asked stiffly, leaving the book untouched on the table.

Tanabe's smile never faltered. "He's a kind of mentor to me. It's impossible to get an appointment with him, but I think he'll be more flexible if it's through me."

"No... I, er..." I shook my head again, then summoned my courage and added, "You're the only one I'm interested in, Tanabe."

"I want you to meet him so that you can get to know me better. His words and way of thinking were a big factor in forming who I am."

I picked up the empty water glass and put it down again. My brain couldn't keep up with what was happening, and I broke out in a cold sweat beneath my blouse. Bracing myself, I looked him straight in his smiling face.

"The app we're registered on is for finding a marriage partner, isn't it?"

"That's right, yes."

"Was that your objective in coming today?"

"Yes," he answered promptly, still smiling. "You're a lovely woman, Hirai. Now that I've met you, I want to cherish this relationship."

It was no good. I decided to stop thinking and focus on how to amicably make an exit. After giving hollow responses to a couple more of his comments, I stood up. "Well, then, I'd better be going." He didn't try to stop me.

As I left, I couldn't resist pushing the book back across the table. "I don't read books like this."

"Well, it'll be your first time, then, won't it?" he responded.

Wordlessly I tossed the shady-looking business book into my work bag, which was large enough to hold A4 documents and completely up swallowed the book.

Rocked by the motion of the train, I held my now heavy bag on my knees. I gazed out of the train window at the buildings of Ikebukuro flashing past, and let my thoughts wander aimlessly. It was just after three on a Saturday afternoon, still too early to go home, and the train was almost empty. A couple opposite me sat with their shoulders touching, peering at the man's phone and whispering together. The girl's bare legs extending from her short skirt were dazzling.

Maybe it was a pyramid scheme. Tanabe's toothy smile resurfaced in my mind, like mud stirred up from a river bottom. It must have been a trick to get me involved in one of those pyramid schemes that were all over the internet. He had claimed to be looking for a marriage partner, but the pyramid scheme had probably been his main objective.

The train pulled into a station, and the couple absorbed in the phone turned to look out of the window and hastily stood up. They ran out of the train onto the platform and glanced at each other, laughing.

I stared at my flat, unvarnished nails. As a woman past the generally accepted marriageable age, I was finding the search for a marriage partner even tougher than I'd expected. This sort of thing couldn't be that unusual. Well, there was nothing I could do about it. I'd best forget it as quickly as possible.

The same words were going round and round in my head as the train arrived at my station and I walked back to our apartment.

It was a pyramid scheme, so there was nothing I could have done about it. It wasn't my fault.

The trees lining the street on my route home were lit up in the afternoon sun. Light shone through the overlapping leaves, making them an impossibly bright green. A single pigeon was crossing over the dappled light that poured onto the asphalt.

But was that really true? The heavy, stagnant pus in the very deepest part of the mud at the bottom of the river began to surface. However hard I tried to suppress it, it came flooding out.

Whatever I did, I just didn't like men. Even if Tanabe had been beyond reproach and not trying to get me involved in a pyramid scheme, the fact remained that I had never been attracted to someone of the opposite sex.

The second man I dated had had a gentle smile. He had very properly asked me to go out with him, and we carried on dating without even holding hands for quite some time. The first time I went to his place and he tried to touch me, I'd reflexively pushed him away. He sat with me and rubbed my back as I hyperventilated, a hurt look on his face, but I couldn't help feeling totally grossed out by the gentle heat from the palm of a man's hand.

Neither the pyramid scheme, nor even the size of his shoulder bag or the teeth that showed when he smiled, had anything to do with it. This was my problem.

"Hi, I'm home."

Suganuma was watching TV in the living room. "Hi there," she said turning round, and with a look of surprise added, "oh, did you go to work today?"

"No."

"It's just that you're dressed for it."

I shouldn't have felt disappointed over something like that, but I was quite put out that I had gone to the trouble of wearing the flared skirt only for it to look like a work outfit after all. I gave a self-deprecating smile and shook my head. Suganuma looked at me oddly, her head tilted to one side. I quickly retreated into my room and pulled my loungewear out of the wardrobe.

The pot-au-feu that Suganuma had made was stuffed with a crazy amount of vegetables. As I drank the consommé-flavoured soup, it gradually warmed my stomach. She skewered a wiener sausage on her fork and placed it in her mouth.

"You know how they always weirdly sell wieners at the supermarket in double packs taped together?" she asked, looking at me. "That used to really piss me off when I lived alone. I mean seriously, what is that all about?"

I couldn't say anything in reply. She looked put out at the fact that I hadn't agreed with her, but I kept eating in silence. I bit into a wiener, and juice from the meat spread in my mouth.

"Today I met someone I got to know through a matchmaking app," I said abruptly.

"You what? That's not like you," she said, her eyes widening. She swallowed what was in her mouth, then asked lightly, "How did it go?"

"He tried to get me involved in a pyramid scheme."

She froze for a moment, then grimaced. "That's a bummer. Awful. I can imagine how you feel about that."

The pot-au-feu for two was on the low table with some bowls and a salad. Something abruptly welled up in me as I looked through the steam rising from the pot-au-feu at the figure of my flatmate sitting cross-legged. Before I knew it, words were spilling out of my mouth.

"I've frozen my eggs," I told her. I had no idea why I was coming out with that confession now. "I had them frozen when I turned thirty-five, and I've been renewing the agreement every year since. All I have to do is post them the renewal document every year, and my eggs are preserved."

"I see," Suganuma said quietly.

Now that I'd started laying myself bare, I couldn't stop. "The success rate isn't very high, so they recommend freezing a certain number so that you're pretty much guaranteed to get pregnant, but it's expensive so I only did half that number. I mean, it's all so half-hearted, and every year I think I should just give up. Or rather, I wonder why I can't bring myself to give up. But I've had enough. I'm going to quit flailing around trying to take the usual route to happiness for women in our society. Maybe it'll be so much easier if I just give up?"

Suganuma placed her fork back on the table and sat with her head bowed, thinking. "Why not carry on?" she asked, looking up. "Unless you really can't afford it, or something unavoidable like that, maybe it's best to keep your options open. If you stop now, you might end up regretting it later."

I hadn't been expecting that kind of response from her. She was being somewhat more serious than usual. I returned her gaze.

"Not giving up isn't always the answer, but then sometimes giving up probably isn't, either," she said and picked up her fork as though that was the end of the conversation.

I took a bite of potato in silence. Suganuma hadn't used much salt in her pot-de-feu and it had a mellow flavour.

*

It was now the season for wearing long-sleeved tops. We had just managed to get through the busy period at the end of September, and had lots of free time in our lives again. I was hanging up Suganuma's T-shirts on the balcony, which was bathed in midday sunlight. She was still wearing short-sleeved shirts indoors. It had been raining a lot lately, but today a deep blue sky spread out above our apartment. As I hung the laundry hangers on the pole, the voices of children playing reached me from the street below. I felt a chill in the bottom of my stomach, despite the pleasant day.

Suganuma had been staying out one night a week for over a month now. It had pretty much become the norm for her to stay out Friday night and come back on Saturday. That was all I could think of while I was hanging up the clothes.

Suganuma didn't tell me what she was doing, and I was too scared to ask. But given the way things were going, there could be only one possible reason.

For a while now, every time I got a message from Suganuma letting me know she would be staying out that night, I had been feeling an emotion akin to rage, which had been building up in me little by little. It was an issue that could potentially affect whether we continued to share the apartment, yet she hadn't bothered to tell me about it. It was Saturday, and she hadn't come home last night. Today I would bring it up with her, I resolved to myself as I shook out a blouse.

Suganuma opened the front door, came into the living room and put a shopping bag from the supermarket on the low table.

"There was fifty yen off on bentos, so I bought one for you too, Hirai."

I got up from the sofa and looked her in the face. She took off her jacket and slung it over the back of the sofa. Her thin arms were bare in her short-sleeved T-shirt, and they smelled of an unfamiliar body soap.

"What's up?" she asked, turning to me with a puzzled look on her face.

"So, have you got a boyfriend?"

I'd tried to think of a good way to bring the subject up, but in the end I just got straight to the point. My heart started pounding. It was pulsing so hard I worried it might be visible beneath my sweatshirt.

"I hadn't quite thought of him like that." She touched the nape of her neck and averted her eyes. "I'm not serious about it, you know. And neither is he, given that he's married and just currently stationed away from home."

I felt my body tense up. My brain was having trouble processing all the bits of information in what she'd said. So, she *was* seeing a man? But he was married, and having an affair?

"So it's not anything that's going to affect us sharing the flat."

I was lost for words. I dreaded to think what my face must look like. The distant cheerful voices of the children playing in the street sounded jarring.

Suganuma scratched her head as though embarrassed. "Do you remember that guy we met in the bar in Atami?"

"Huh?" That dirty old man? I barely managed to swallow the words that rose to my throat.

"We exchanged numbers while you were in the toilet. I felt a bit awkward about it so I didn't tell you. Sorry."

"You don't have to apologize," I answered, mentally drawing a picture of the man I'd seen in Atami. He'd had a big nose, glittering eyes against dark skin. An intense feeling of disgust started creeping up from my feet, like that time when I was fifteen and had seen Masatoshi for the first time. "But what are you going to do? Especially if you get pregnant," I said a little too forcefully to cover up the fact my voice was trembling.

"I won't get pregnant."

She clearly enunciated each syllable, as if talking down to a child.

"You won't get pregnant?" I parroted senselessly.

"No, I won't," she said quietly but firmly.

It felt like she was being dismissive.

"Well, if you say so." Even to my ears, the tone of my voice sounded unconvincing.

*

There was a lively atmosphere in the izakaya by the west exit of Yokohama Station. The servers in Japanese-style uniforms were rushed off their feet. We were shown through to a table for six and we ordered our drinks while we browsed the sticky menu. The place was known for its semi-private rooms, with tables separated by walls and bamboo blinds, and the interior design was uniformly black. It wasn't black out of any sense of style, it was just the easy option that also helpfully covered up the grime.

We had just finished the accounts for the quarter to end September, and Mrs Kondo had suggested we go out to celebrate. An office junior was tasked with organizing it, and the six people from our section would attend. "You've been working really hard too,

Hirai, so you must come," Mrs Kondo insisted. "I'll make sure it's on a day that works for you, Hirai-san," the office junior added, effectively leaving me no room to refuse. It was the first work party I'd attended for several years.

After we'd raised our glasses for kanpai, we all sat in silence picking at the small dish that had come with our drinks. I slowly chewed on the rather bland hijiki seaweed and did my best not to catch anyone's eye.

Surprisingly, it was Yoshida who was the first to break the ice.

"So, it seems we won't be doing that any more in our company then, doesn't it?"

Mrs Kondo looked at him questioningly. "Doing what?"

"Working from home."

"Aahh!"

This exaggerated reaction set everyone off, and they all stopped eating to start commenting noisily.

"My friend says that in their company they're working more from home now as a result of Covid."

"It's good for people with kids, right?"

"No way—working at home if you've got a toddler around is impossible. Totally out of the question."

"It's actually going to be tougher if they start expecting us to raise kids at home even if both partners work!"

"My son is already in elementary school, so I'm happy if it means I don't have to leave him in after-school programmes. Of course, I feel less anxious being at home together with him."

"Anyway, half of accounts work can be done at home. Especially now we have the CIE Tech system installed."

"I wish the top brass at our company would consider it."

I understood the sentiment of being envious of others working from home, but I didn't know where to insert myself into the conversation. I was putting all my effort into appearing engaged and as though I was participating, when Mrs Kondo suddenly changed the subject.

"Come to think of it, Hirai, tell me more about the person you mentioned a while ago."

Abruptly, the other four all turned their gazes to me.

"You mean my flatmate?"

"Yes, yes... I had no idea!"

Everyone other than Mrs Kondo was looking mystified.

I'd thought this topic would probably come up, but I hadn't been able to decide how to deal with it. Mrs Kondo was sitting diagonally opposite, smiling and looking expectantly at me. I looked down at my glass of cassis-orange and forced a smile.

"Um, when I said I lived with someone, I forgot to mention it was with a woman."

Mrs Kondo's expression froze, her smile still in place. My colleagues' hands also halted midair with their drinks, and it was as though our table alone had been visited by a silence that cut us off from the noisy bustle of the rest of the izakaya. I didn't meet anyone's eyes, but I could feel their curious gazes criss-crossing above my head. They were probably wondering what I'd meant by living with a woman.

"Oh, it's not like she's my partner or anything!" I added hastily. "We just share a flat, that's all."

As the atmosphere eased slightly, Mrs Kondo smiled a little too broadly.

"Ah, um, I see. So that's how it is. Ugh, I jumped to the wrong conclusion, didn't I? I'm sorry."

"No, it's okay... it's normal to think that. I know it's unusual at my age."

"Not at all," Mrs Kondo said flatly, the corners of her mouth gradually coming down. She didn't say any more, and gulped down some of her large glass of beer as if to fill the gap. Sitting next to her, the office junior reached with his chopsticks for some food and said nonchalantly, "When my wife was still single she used to share a flat too."

"Really? Maybe it's a bit more common these days."

"Oh, by the way, I often talk about work at home, and my wife says she'd love to meet you sometime, Mrs Kondo."

"What? I don't believe you! What on earth have you been telling her?"

Now the flow of conversation was picking up. Once the topic had been quickly and discreetly redirected, the tension eased around the table. Once again I devoted myself to making innocuous interjections.

Out in the dark street, I stepped over the asphalt in my pumps. The night breeze caressing my cheeks, no longer flushed with alcohol, was cold.

On the surface of it, the drinks party had ended congenially, and Mrs Kondo had apparently gone on to another bar with some of the office juniors for more drinks. They were probably gossiping about me right now, or otherwise pretending that nothing had happened.

Who cares, I thought. The traffic light changed for the road on my left, and several cars set off all at once.

Maybe I should get in touch with that pyramid scheme guy Tanabe after all. Even if the worst happened and we ended up divorcing, at least I could maybe have a go at having a child.

The moment I thought of it, I knew that it wasn't the answer I was looking for. How could I even have considered it? I wasn't even sure whether I really wanted to give birth to another human being, or how much of a responsibility raising them would be. But that thought was somehow stuck in my head. Where on earth had this desire to have a child come from?

When I got home, I dashed into my room before having to face Suganuma. I threw down my bag and lay on the bed. The stale smell of the izakaya had seeped into my clothes and hair and suddenly asserted itself.

As always, I closed my eyes and held my breath. I stiffened my body, focusing my awareness right up to the tips of my fingers and toes. *I am dead.*

In spite of myself, Tanabe's face floated through my mind and I couldn't get rid of it. Eventually, I could no longer bear to be still anymore. My left hand, flung out in front of me, finally flinched.

I sat up and now felt a fierce energy well up in me. I had to be doing something, or I would be dragged into something truly horrifying. I took my phone out of my bag. The rectangular liquid crystal screen glowed in the dark room. I opened up the LINE chat history with Tanabe for the first time in two months, and saw that numerous unread messages were waiting for me. I ran my eyes over the oldest message.

<Good evening! Do you like sports, Hirai? It feels great to move your body, you know. Me and a group of friends are going to hold a futsal match soon, so how about joining us? We're only doing it for fun, so it's totally fine if you've never done it before (^^♪>

The next message was an invitation to a cooking class, and the one after that to a beer garden. After that were unabashed invitations to a seminar and dinner with the person he considered a "teacher", and the last one was to a BBQ.

The knuckle of my index finger was lit up by the screen. The messages had arrived at the rate of about one a week, with a variety of proposals, and all composed in the same upbeat tone. Where were Tanabe's feelings? He had sent all these messages to me, but I had the feeling none of them were actually directed at me. Listed there on the screen, they all looked relentlessly hollow. As I traced them with my finger, I was suddenly flooded with a bitterness I couldn't let pass. My phone slipped from my hand and bounced on the bed. It wasn't possible to give up everything and keep on living without feeling pain. Hit by the full realization of what had always been obvious, I curled my body up into a ball.

The living-room light was on when I came out of my bedroom. I took a few unsteady steps towards it, like a plant instinctively reaching its leaves out to the sun. I somehow hadn't considered the possibility that Suganuma might be there, but of course when I opened the door there she was, standing in the corner of the room. Her hands were busy doing something on the 3D printer.

After a few moments, the printer screeched into action. Suganuma turned round and tilted her head at me standing there by the door.

"I'm sorry, is the noise bothering you? If I don't work through the night I might miss my deadline."

I shook my head without saying anything. The noise didn't bother me at all. Right now I wanted the sound and brightness of a human presence other than myself to fill the room.

"Hirai, is there anything you want me to make for you?" Suganuma asked out of the blue as she watched the object being moulded on the 3D printer's base.

"What?"

"It's your birthday soon. As long as the printer can do it I'll make whatever you like—it'll be good practice for me."

Something I wanted. I thought hard. What immediately rose up in my mind were soft curves. Soft, warm, and fragile.

"Can you make a baby?"

Suganuma looked up. She put her hand to her jaw, as if in thought.

"A baby—what a good idea. Quite tricky... it'll be good practice." Her eyes sparkled as she went on cheerfully, "There is a size limit, so would a newborn be okay?"

She was simply interested in the art of printing, and I felt none of the nosiness my colleagues had shown earlier. I nodded, and thanked her.

The screech of the printer rang out loud in the night as we sat in the room for a while longer, talking about the design of the baby.

The next day was Saturday, and it was past noon when I woke up. When I was younger I'd always felt irritated at having wasted a day, but not now. It was said that people woke up earlier as they aged whether they wanted to or not, and the thought made me want to savour this pleasantly languorous feeling while I still could.

When I went into the living room, I saw the figure of a baby in the box of rejects to burn at the shrine. I gently picked up the white plastic doll. Like the dogs, it was hollow inside and very light. Its puffy eyes were closed and its little hands were clenched in front of its body. Upon closer inspection I saw that its legs were fused together, and it didn't have enough toes. Still, it looked very much like a baby. It even had thin hairs moulded one by one on its head.

I turned the baby on its side and held it to my breast the way you often see in pictures of mothers. My gaze was drawn to the face resting in the crook of my arm. Its eyes were closed, but I had the pleasant feeling that it was looking at me, and I started trembling with joy.

My baby. Hollow inside, misshapen, defective. It was perfect for me. It fit so snugly in my arms.

I'd been holding it like this for a while when Suganuma came into the living room. For a moment she looked tense, then immediately started checking us over with the critical gaze she used for her work.

"That one's a dud, you know. If you wait a little I'll make a proper—"

"No, I like this one."

Suganuma looked doubtful, but seeing me gazing in silence at the baby in my arms, she suddenly lowered her voice and asked, "Doesn't it make you want a baby? A real one?"

"No. I have this one, and it's enough for me."

She looked puzzled.

"I know it's weird." I myself had never expected to feel such contentment from something like this.

Gently, I put the baby down on the sofa. Its rounded back wasn't stable, and it toppled over. Suganuma looked at it lying there and tilted her head, dissatisfied.

"Well, if you're really happy with it, then I guess it's okay. Although I do wish you'd let me play around with it a bit more."

I threw the business book from Tanabe and the white envelope into the box of rejects to burn at the shrine. The envelope contained the renewal papers for the contract to keep my eggs frozen. I told Suganuma that the box was getting full, and she said that she also had a lot of finished pieces ready to send, and eagerly set about packing everything up ready for collection.

The two boxes, one of completed dog figurines and the other of duds to burn at the shrine, sat side by side in the hall. The contents of one would go back home to their owners, while those in the other would be consigned to oblivion without ever reaching their owners or even coming into existence. Suganuma knelt before the boxes and held her hands together in prayer, so I followed suit. I didn't know what to pray for. My eggs would never develop into a person, and I thought it would be good if they could go to the same place as the beloved dogs that had died, and their spirits could live on together wagging their tails.

JAPANESE FICTION AVAILABLE AND COMING SOON FROM PUSHKIN PRESS

MS ICE SANDWICH
Mieko Kawakami

MURDER IN THE AGE OF ENLIGHTENMENT
Ryūnosuke Akutagawa

THE HONJIN MURDERS
Seishi Yokomizo

RECORD OF A NIGHT TOO BRIEF
Hiromi Kawakami

SPRING GARDEN
Tomoka Shibasaki

COIN LOCKER BABIES
Ryu Murakami

THE DECAGON HOUSE MURDERS
Yukito Ayatsuji

SLOW BOAT
Hideo Furukawa

THE HUNTING GUN
Yasushi Inoue

SALAD ANNIVERSARY
Machi Tawara

THE CAKE TREE IN THE RUINS
Akiyuki Nosaka